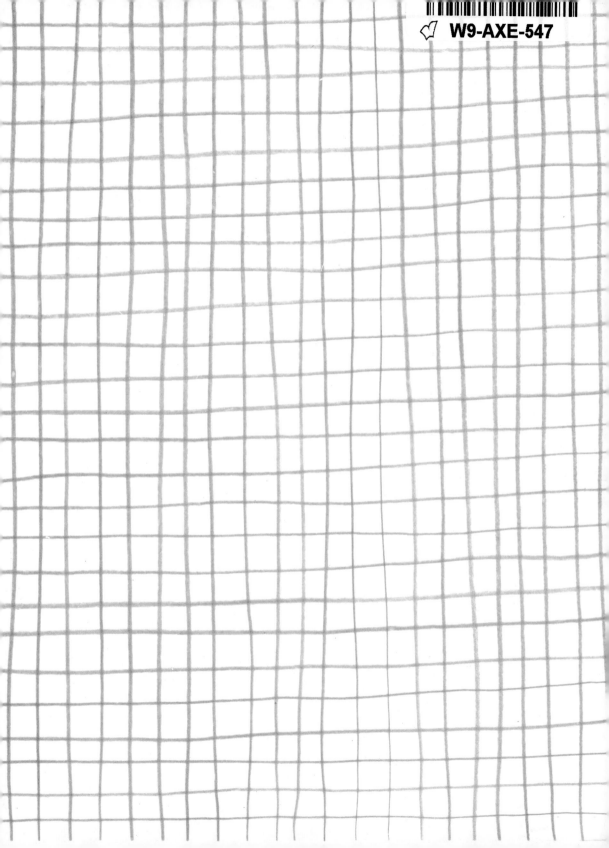

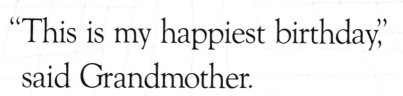

"This is my happiest birthday,"
said Grandmother.

Grandmother hugged and kissed him. She had tears in her eyes.

"I wrote it all by myself, Grandma," said Edward.

"I have a poem for your birthday, Grandma," said Edward. "Here it is."

We love visiting you, Grandma.
We love the smell of your house, Grandma.
Grandma, we love your apple cookies.
Grandma, we love your blueberry jam.
We love the way you spoil us, Grandma.
We love your stories, Grandma.
Grandma, we love your backrubs.
Grandma, we love it when you let us stay up late.
We love your pretty pink apron, Grandma.
We love how you comb out your long, white hair
*   at night, Grandma.*
But especially, we love you, Grandma.
Happy birthday, dear Grandma,
*   happy birthday to you.*

For her birthday, Elizabeth gave
Grandmother a lavender sachet,
a pair of potholders, a basket,
a fluffy pillow, a book end,
a soap dish, a lamp shade, wrapping
paper and a knitted headband.

Grandmother hugged and kissed her.
She had tears in her eyes.

"I made everything myself, Grandma",
said Elizabeth.

"What are you making Grandmother for her birthday?" asked Elizabeth.

"It's a secret," replied Edward.

"I love how Grandmother combs out her long, white hair at night," said Elizabeth.

"Are you knitting a headband for her birthday?" asked Edward.

"It's a secret," replied Elizabeth.

"I love Grandmother's pretty pink apron", said Elizabeth.

"Are you making pink wrapping paper for her birthday?" asked Edward.

"It's a secret", replied Elizabeth.

"I love it when Grandmother lets us stay up late," said Elizabeth.

"Are you making a lamp shade for her birthday?" asked Edward.

"It's a secret," replied Elizabeth.

"I love Grandmother's backrubs," said Elizabeth.

"Are you making a soap dish for her birthday?" asked Edward.

"It's a secret," replied Elizabeth.

"I love Grandmother's stories," said Elizabeth.

"Are you making a book end for her birthday?" asked Edward.

"It's a secret," replied Elizabeth.

"I love the way Grandmother spoils us," said Elizabeth.

"Are you making a fluffy pillow for her birthday?" asked Edward.

"It's a secret," replied Elizabeth.

"I love Grandmother's blueberry jam," said Elizabeth.

"Are you making a basket for her birthday?" asked Edward.

"It's a secret," replied Elizabeth.

"I love Grandmother's apple cookies," said Elizabeth.

"Are you making potholders for her birthday?" asked Edward.

"It's a secret," replied Elizabeth.

"I love the smell of Grandmother's house," said Elizabeth.

"Are you making a lavender sachet for her birthday?" asked Edward.

"It's a secret," replied Elizabeth.

"I love visiting Grandmother,"
said Elizabeth.

"It's her birthday next month,"
said Edward. "What are you
making for her?"

"It's a secret," replied Elizabeth.

for Yiayiá and Grossmutter

This book is a presentation of Newfield Publications, Inc.
Newfield Publications offers book clubs for children
from preschool through high school. For further
information write to: **Newfield Publications, Inc.,**
4343 Equity Drive, Columbus, Ohio 43228.

Edited for and published by arrangement with
Greenwillow Books, a division of William Morrow & Company, Inc.

Newfield Publications is a federally registered trademark of
Newfield Publications, Inc. Weekly Reader is a federally
registered trademark of Weekly Reader Corporation.

Library of Congress Cataloging in Publication Data
Brandenberg, Franz, A secret for grandmother's birthday.
SUMMARY: A brother and sister cat plan the secret gifts
they will give grandmother cat for her birthday.
[1. Grandmothers—Fiction. 2. Birthdays—Fiction] I. Aliki. II. Title.
PZ7.B7364Se [E] 75-10606 ISBN 0-688-80012-2 ISBN 0-688-84012-4 lib. bdg.
ISBN 0-688-05781-0 (1985 Printing) ISBN 0-688-05782-9 lib. bdg. (1985 Printing)

Weekly Reader Children's Book Club Presents

A Secret for Grandmother's Birthday

by Franz Brandenberg • illustrated by Aliki

Greenwillow Books

A Division of William Morrow & Company, Inc. / New York